The Doomsday Virus

by

Steve Barlow

and

Steve Skidmore

Illustrated by Harriet Buckley

Find out more about
Steve Barlow and Steve Skidmore at
www.the2steves.net

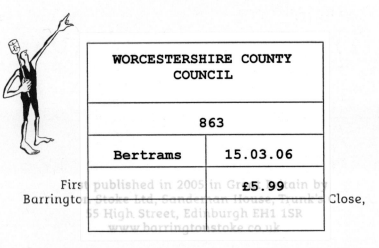

First published in 2005 in Great Britain by
Barrington Stoke Ltd, Sandeman House, Trunk's Close,
55 High Street, Edinburgh EH1 1SR
www.barringtonstoke.co.uk

ISBN 1-842992-88-0

Printed in Great Britain by Bell & Bain Ltd

Barrington Stoke gratefully acknowledges support from the
Scottish Arts Council towards the publication of the
fyi series

Scottish
Arts Council
LOTTERY FUNDED

Contents

Chapter 1
The Prisoner

"Behind that door is the most dangerous criminal on this planet."

Agent Makepeace pointed a dramatic finger at the shining steel door. Doctor Lee gave a sigh. Makepeace was just like any other agent from the Central Security Agency – a show-off. And why did they always wear dark suits? Who did they think they were, the Men In Black?

"So where are the guards?" asked Doctor Lee.

Agent Makepeace shook his head. "We don't need them. No-one can escape from here. It's the most secure cell in the CSA."

"And how do we get in?"

The agent pointed at a small LCD unit on the wall.

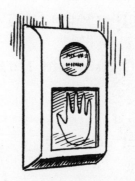

"A DNA scanner. There's one inside as well. You place your hand on the sensor and it checks your identity with the Central Security Agency database. If the scan doesn't come up with a match, it hits you with 60,000 volts of electricity. Zap!"

The Doctor raised an eyebrow.

Agent Makepeace grinned. "It's all right, the system has been programmed to recognise your DNA. Anyway, the shock isn't strong enough to kill you. Just enough to stop you going anywhere for a while."

"And has anyone ever escaped?"

"No-one. The system is foolproof. No two people have the same DNA make-up."

"I know that, Agent Makepeace. I am a doctor."

"I thought you were a computer doctor."

"The links between computers and humans are closer than you think," replied Doctor Lee. "Can we go in?"

Makepeace frowned. "You know I object to this meeting. Corder is dangerous."

"The Director over-ruled you," said the Doctor. "We need him. He's the only one who can help us. I'm sure your security is fine. Even Corder can't change his DNA."

Makepeace said nothing and placed his hand against the sensor. Seconds later, it flashed green and the door slid open. He went through and the door closed.

Doctor Lee then placed her hand on the DNA scanner. She felt a tingling on her skin. The door opened. She stepped through and it shut behind her.

The Doctor had not expected the prison cell to be so bare. Steel walls, a bed with white sheets and a pillow, a toilet and sink, a table and two chairs. And sitting on one of the chairs was "the most dangerous criminal on the planet" – a thin, dark-haired, 14-year-old boy.

Chapter 2
The Hacker

The boy looked up.

"Tim Corder?"

The teenager looked slowly around the room. "There doesn't seem to be anyone else here. So I must be."

"Watch what you say, Corder," Makepeace raised his fist and moved forward. The doctor held up her hand to stop him.

"May I sit down?" she asked, pointing at the empty chair.

Tim gave her a half smile. "Be my guest."

Placing her black computer case and an orange file on the table, Doctor Lee sat down. Tim glanced at the cover of the file:

"So, how are you, Tim?"

"I'm locked in here on my own 24/7. No visits or calls, no contact with family or friends. Not even a mouse for company." He nodded towards the Doctor's case. "Let alone a computer. How do you think I am?" His eyes narrowed. "Anyway, I'm sure you're not here to worry about how I'm feeling. Why don't you get to the point?"

"OK. My name is Doctor Lee. I work for a government department dealing with world-wide Internet security. We need your help."

Tim said nothing.

The Doctor opened up the file and began to read:

Tim Corder. Age 14.

Also known by the names of Hack-Jack, AK48, Kordyte. Dangerous computer terrorist.

During his short hacking career, Tim Corder has managed to crack the top security systems of every secret service in the world: CIA, MI6, FSB, Mossad.

Tim Corder was arrested just before he was going to transfer money from the top 50 companies in the world into charity accounts.

She put the file down. "Very impressive."

"A real Robin Hood," sneered Agent
Makepeace. Tim gave him a look of pure
hate.

"Many people might say that what Tim
was doing was a good thing, Agent," said
Doctor Lee.

"It was a criminal act," said Makepeace. "That's why he's here."

The Doctor flicked over a page. "It says in your file that your partner, code-named Zeen, has never been caught." She closed the file and stared at Tim.

"You think I'm going to tell you Zeen's real name?"

The Doctor shook her head. "No – and I'm not going to ask."

"So why are you here?"

"You're clever, Tim. Maybe even a genius. That's why you've been locked away here with no access to a computer. Someone like you is a danger to the whole planet. But you could also be helpful. We need you. There's a computer virus out there."

"There are always viruses on the Web – thousands of them," said Tim.

"This one is different," replied the Doctor. "This is the big one. The one you hackers have talked about for a long time. This is the Doomsday virus. When it goes on the attack, it will destroy the Internet and every computer network on this planet."

"Sweet," said Tim. "So what's this got to do with me?"

"We think you're the only person in the world who can stop it."

Chapter 3
The Worm

Tim stared at Doctor Lee. "What makes you think I can help you? Even if I wanted to?"

Makepeace pointed a finger in Tim's face. "Don't think you're the only one working on this, big shot," he snapped. "We've got *real* experts on the case."

Tim stared back. "But they haven't cracked it, or you wouldn't be here," he pointed out.

Makepeace glared and said nothing.

Tim turned to Doctor Lee. "And what if I do help you? What's in it for me?"

The Doctor glanced at Makepeace, who gave an angry nod.

"If you break the source code," she said, "we will offer you your freedom."

"What?" said Tim. "I walk out of here? Just like that?"

"No," snarled Makepeace, "not 'just like that'! You'll be watched! And if you ever try to programme anything more complex than an alarm clock you'll be back in here so fast your pants will catch fire!"

There was a moment's silence as Tim thought about this. At last he nodded. "Tell me about it."

The Doctor unzipped her computer case, pulled out a state-of-the-art laptop and switched it on. Tim's eyes flashed.

"Two days ago," said Doctor Lee, "the CSA received an e-mail with a warning that a worm was going to be released onto the Web. We don't know who sent it."

The Doctor turned the computer's screen to face Tim. "This is it."

Doctor Lee waited for Tim to react, but he just shrugged.

"Don't you get it, kid?" said Makepeace. "Today is the fourth."

"Is it? I lose track of time in here." Tim showed the agent his left wrist. "And I haven't got a watch, either. It was taken away."

The Doctor gave Tim a look. "It's now 17.00 hours. We have two hours before the worm is released."

"Is that all?" said Tim. "You'd better tell me more."

"The attachment on the e-mail was the worm itself – code-named Doomsday," Doctor Lee told him. "It wasn't a live worm – it was just the source code."

Tim looked puzzled. "Nobody gives a warning that they're going to release a worm onto the Web, they just do it. It's no fun if people know it's coming – unless this is some kind of blackmail?"

Makepeace shook his head. "There haven't been any demands for money."

"Then it's a hoax? Someone having you on?"

"We did think it might be that at first," said Doctor Lee. "We got our experts onto it. They ran tests to see how great the threat was. They found out that Doomsday will act like any other worm infection on a computer. Like a human virus that passes from person to person, this is going to pass itself from computer to computer. It's a small piece of code that will get into a computer, copy itself, then automatically send itself onto other machines."

"No problem then," said Tim. "Just write a security patch that people can download onto their computers to protect them against the worm."

"Do you think we haven't thought of that?" sneered Makepeace.

Doctor Lee shook her head. "We've never seen anything like this coding before. It breaks all the rules of programming. If this worm is released into the wild, it will make the Code Red, Bagel, Netsky and Sasser worms look like Wiggly-woo."

Makepeace frowned. "Wiggly-woo?"

Doctor Lee gave a sigh. "It's a children's song, Makepeace – *There's a worm at the bottom of my garden, and his name is Wiggly-woo ...*"

Makepeace stared at her. "Has that got anything to do with our problem?"

The Doctor took no notice. "Doomsday could cause even more damage than the Slammer worm."

"The one that caused the power blackouts in America?" said Tim.

"That's top secret information," snapped Makepeace. "How do *you* know the blackouts were caused by the Slammer worm?"

Tim gave Makepeace a look of contempt. "I just know."

"The Doomsday worm will search the Web and try to infect any of the world's four billion IP addresses. Once it gets into a computer, it will turn the machine into a slave. This zombie computer will then try and infect other machines. The more computers that get infected, the more messages will be sent and the more worms will be created. Doomsday has the power to breed at an amazing rate. We have worked out that it will double itself every two seconds ..."

Tim nodded. "Which will cause the route Domain Name Servers in the world to overload ..."

"... And crash the whole of the Internet in less than ten minutes."

"Now, that *is* a problem."

"No," said Doctor Lee. "That's only *part* of the problem ..."

Chapter 4
The Virus

"Let me guess," said Tim. "The worm has got a virus attached to it?"

"Correct," replied Doctor Lee. "The same day we got the Doomsday worm, a CD arrived in the post." She reached over and tapped at the keys. Another message appeared on the computer screen:

"So when the worm hits a machine," said Tim, "the virus will arrive as well. What will it do?"

"The virus will download itself onto the computer's hard drive. We ran it on a test machine that wasn't linked to any network. It destroyed everything. If this virus gets out, the programme is so destructive that it will delete all stored information, disable applications and erase the hard drives of every computer it infects."

"It sounds like a Trojan horse," said Tim.

"What's a Trojan horse?" asked Makepeace. Tim rolled his eyes.

"It's a computer programme," said Doctor Lee. "It pretends to be something it's not. It gets into a computer and fools the user into opening it up by pretending to be an important message or document."

"But a virus can only infect a machine if it's activated," said Tim. "The computer user has to open up the virus to make it run. That's part of the challenge for the virus writer – how to fool the person into opening up the programme."

"Doomsday is different," Doctor Lee told him. "The coding on the worm fools the *computer* itself into activating the virus programme. It'll get past any virus protection software and get through every firewall we have. No system is going to be safe: Windows, Mac OS, UNIX – they're all going to be hit."

"I suppose turning off the main Internet hub servers is out of the question?"

"Switch off the entire net?" Doctor Lee shook her head. "The modern world can't exist without it. And what happens when

we turn the Web back on? Doomsday will still be there ..."

Tim gave a low whistle. "Wow! A double whammy! The Doomsday worm crashes the Internet, and the Doomsday virus trashes all the data on every machine. Sweet!"

"Sweet! Is that what you think?" Makepeace exploded with fury. "What sort of sick person are you? Everything that depends on computers will fail. There'll be no mobile phones. No banks. No transport. No satellites, and without satellites to help them navigate, oil tankers will run aground and planes will drop out of the sky."

Makepeace jabbed a finger in Tim's chest. "But that's just for starters. Power stations will shut off. No electricity, gas or water. Without supermarket computers to order food, the shelves will be empty. People will riot. And who'll take care of that? The army, the police, the fire and ambulance services will be unable to move. Defence systems will think they've been attacked and fire nuclear missiles, which will make other countries fire back!" Makepeace glared at Tim, breathing hard. "Doesn't the end of the world matter to you?"

"I'm locked up in this room. Why should it?"

Makepeace moved towards Tim.

"Back off, Makepeace," warned Doctor Lee. "Tim, if you break this source code and write a security patch to stop Doomsday, you'll be set free. The Director has promised." She pushed the computer towards him. "The worm and virus programmes are in here. Please?"

Tim reached for the laptop and began tapping at the keys. Doctor Lee and Makepeace looked on in silence.

Minutes passed before Tim spoke. "The virus is poly-morphic."

"Oh no," whispered Doctor Lee. "Then we're finished."

Chapter 5
The Code

Makepeace stared at her. "Finished? Why?"

"A poly-morphic virus means that every time the worm sends itself to another machine, it changes its code," said Doctor Lee. "Security patches only work if they know what they're looking for. If the code is never the same, the worm will always get past them."

"Maybe not," said Tim. "If I can see how the code changes when it is sent to a computer, I might be able to come up with something. But this laptop isn't networked. I'll need to connect it to a network to see what happens to the code."

Makepeace let out a cry. "Connect it to the net? No way."

Tim shrugged. "Then I can't help you. Like you said – it's the end of the world."

"Agent Makepeace!" Doctor Lee's voice was sharp. "I must remind you, the Director instructed you to offer me every co-operation. *Every* co-operation."

"You don't have to connect me to the Web," Tim said. "Just your internal network. You can isolate it from the Web while I'm working, if you don't trust me."

"You can't connect to our intranet in here," said Makepeace. "There's no line into this cell."

Doctor Lee pointed to her laptop. "This machine has wireless technology. It will connect via radio waves. All you have to do is take the CSA network offline and connect this machine to it. Time is ticking away. Do it now, Agent."

Makepeace turned his back and flipped open his phone.

As he snapped out orders, the Doctor spoke to Tim in a low voice, "Can you stop Doomsday? Really?"

"I'll give it my best shot, Doc."

Makepeace flipped his phone shut. "You have access to the internal network," he said.

The Doctor stroked the laptop's touchpad. She right-clicked and the Central Security Agency logo flashed up on the screen. She passed the computer back to Tim.

Tim's fingers danced over the keyboard. "I'm going to try to crack the code for the worm. That's the most important thing. Without the worm, the virus has no means of transport, so it can't spread."

A box appeared. It filled with flowing lines of code, flashing and changing so quickly that Doctor Lee was unable to follow them.

Makepeace stared at the screen. "It's just numbers ... symbols ... how can junk like this mess up the whole Internet?"

"Computers work with this 'junk'." Tim's eyes never left the screen. "And infecting someone else's machine is easy."

Makepeace gave him a nasty look. "How come?"

"People are lazy," said Tim, "or ignorant – usually both. It's easy to stop viruses. You can buy software protection – but that only works on viruses that were around when it was written. There are always new viruses turning up, so you have to keep updating the software through downloads, but people don't bother."

"They wouldn't need to," Makepeace told him, "if punks like you didn't keep messing around with computers."

"It's human nature," said Doctor Lee. "The minute someone makes something, someone else has to work out a way to break it. Hackers see it as a game. They try to write new worms and viruses faster than software companies can write security patches for them. That's why it's a bad idea to run a programme from a source you don't know. And opening any e-mail attachment can be risky, and if it's an executable the risks are even greater. Even if you know the person sending it, you don't know whether their machine's been infected. *They* may not know it has. You could let in a Trojan horse."

"Thanks for the advice." Makepeace took Doctor Lee by the arm and led her into a corner of the room where Tim couldn't hear them. "What I need to know from you right now is: can the kid really crack this code?"

Doctor Lee shook her head. "I don't know. He lost me quite a while ago. He's working at levels I can't understand."

Makepeace ground his teeth. "I don't trust him."

"We have to trust him," said Doctor Lee. "I don't know if he can stop Doomsday. But I do know that if he can't, no-one can."

Chapter 6
The Patch

Time passed. Makepeace prowled around the room like a caged tiger. He loosened his tie, then undid the top button of his shirt. He checked his watch. "30 minutes."

Doctor Lee kept her eyes on the screen, trying to follow what Tim was doing as he checked and cross-checked codes. Every now and then, she understood for a moment what he was doing but seconds later, Tim would lose her again.

"15 minutes," Makepeace said. "You're running out of time."

"Tim?" Doctor Lee looked worried.

"I'm cool." Tim didn't look cool. He looked as if the stress was getting to him, but his fingers never stopped in their search.

"Ten minutes." Makepeace ran his fingers through his hair and swore. "This is going nowhere."

"Come on, Tim," muttered Doctor Lee, "nail that worm."

"I'm working on it."

There was a long silence.

Makepeace said, "Three minutes."

The codes stopped rolling across the screen. Tim looked up. "It's done. The software patch for Doomsday is ready for release. It will kill the worm and stop the virus getting out. All you have to do is reconnect your network to the Web right now and let it go."

"Just a minute," Makepeace shook his head. "How can we trust you? It's too risky."

"What happens if we don't?" snapped Doctor Lee. "Doomsday? Give the order now!"

Makepeace spoke into his phone.

Doctor Lee snatched her computer back and clicked on the Internet browser. She gave a sigh of relief as it opened up. She looked at Tim.

Tim nodded. "Press 'send'."

Doctor Lee's finger stabbed at the key.

Makepeace flicked his phone shut and checked his watch. "30 seconds."

The Doctor typed an address. A picture appeared on the screen.

"This shows the state of the Web," she said. She pointed. "The lines show traffic, the blinking dots are hubs. If the lines

break and the dots go out, the worm has worked and the Net is down."

In a hoarse voice, Makepeace said, "19.00 hours. Doomsday."

Nothing happened.

Nothing continued to happen. The lines continued to glow, the hubs continued to blink.

Doctor Lee breathed, "He's done it."

Chapter 7
The Lie

Doctor Lee turned to Tim. "You did it!"

"Sure I did." Tim leaned back and clasped his hands behind his head. "You said it yourself, Doc. I'm the best!"

Makepeace snorted.

Tim pointed at the Doctor's laptop. "I'm sure your experts will be able to come up with a security update for the virus, just in case it gets released on the Web some other way. If you have a problem, just get in touch."

"Thank you, Mr Corder." Doctor Lee shut down the laptop and slipped it back into its case. She smiled at Tim. "Can I get you anything?"

"No," snapped Makepeace, "you can't."

Tim gave Doctor Lee a twisted smile. "Chill out, Doc. Anyhow, I'll be out of here soon."

"Why, yes, that's right." Doctor Lee gave Tim a half smile. "Goodbye, then ..."

She crossed to the door and placed her palm against the DNA reader. After a few seconds, the door opened. The Doctor went out. The door closed.

Tim gave Makepeace a friendly grin. "So, when do I check out?"

Makepeace returned the grin with a sneer. "You don't."

Tim's face became hard. "What do you mean? You said if I cracked Doomsday, you'd let me go."

"I lied." Makepeace smiled. "Sue me."

Tim stared at him and said nothing.

"You fool!" snarled Makepeace. "Did you really believe the CSA would let you go? You've just shown why we'd be crazy to do that! If we let you loose, there'd soon be another bug out there, ten times worse than Doomsday. And you wouldn't be stopping it, you'd be sending it! Nothing doing, wise guy. You'll stay in here until you rot!"

Chapter 8
The Switch

Makepeace turned and marched to the door. He put his hand on the DNA scanner.

There was a flash. Blue lines of electric force crackled and sparked around Makepeace. They wrapped him in a moving, clinging web of energy. The agent gave a cry. His body went stiff. His eyes glazed over.

The electric field snapped off. Makepeace fell to the floor and lay still.

"Oops," said Tim. He got up from his chair and crossed the room. He bent down over Agent Makepeace.

"I know you can hear me," he said.

Makepeace said nothing. He couldn't. But his eyes moved, fixing themselves on Tim.

"I thought you might go back on your word. So I had a back-up plan. You were right not to trust me. You should never have let me into the CSA network. Of course, you had no choice. But in fact it only took me a few seconds to rewrite the codes to stop the Doomsday worm. Would you like to know what I was doing the rest of the time?"

Makepeace's eyes flashed angrily.

"I was hacking into your server," Tim went on. "I changed a few details. I told the database that my DNA code was yours – and yours was mine. So when you used the scanner just now, it thought you were me, trying to escape. Kapow!"

Makepeace bared his teeth in a silent snarl.

Tim put his hand inside Makepeace's jacket and took out his mobile phone. He dialled a number. "Hi. It's Tim. The plan worked." He listened to the phone for a while. "Got you. OK. See you later." He snapped the phone shut, and grinned at Makepeace. "Mind if I hang on to this?"

The agent was turning red with fury.

"You see," said Tim, "I was able to stop Doomsday because I wrote it." He shrugged. "Well, co-wrote it. With Zeen. That was him on the phone, by the way. We had a plan that, if either of us were caught, the other would threaten to let loose the Doomsday worm. Zeen sent you the e-mail and the CD. We knew Doctor Lee's people wouldn't be able to fix it. Sooner or later you'd *have* to call me in. And once you'd let me into your system, I was home free."

Makepeace was made of stern stuff. He managed to gasp out, "Guards ... will ... stop ... you ..."

Tim shook his head. "No guards. The system is foolproof, remember?" He stood up. "The shock will wear off, soon. You'll be able to move again. Feel free to shout and kick the walls as much as you want. I did plenty of that when I first got here. It won't work of course. This cell is soundproof, in case you've forgotten."

Tim took the watch from Makepeace's arm and put it on his own. "Someone will bring you breakfast in ..." He checked the time. "11 hours and 37 minutes – the service is always on time around here. Of course, by then I'll be long gone. Zeen fixed an airline ticket for me – in a false name." He winked at Makepeace. "An electronic ticket, of course."

Makepeace swore.

Tim gave him a friendly pat on the cheek. "Don't feel too bad. Tell you what – the next virus we create, we'll name it after you. The Makepeace Virus. Coming soon, to a PC near you. How'd you like that?" Makepeace shook with rage. "Hey, calm

down. Think of your blood pressure." Tim
winked. "See you around."

He crossed the cell to the DNA reader,
and pressed his palm against the screen.
The door opened. Tim stepped through.

He walked briskly down the long
corridors of the Central Security Agency. At
every locked door, his DNA was scanned.
The CSA people did not even look at him.
He couldn't be an intruder. The system was
foolproof.

Tim arrived at the last door. Outside there were trees and grass. A flag snapped in the breeze. Cars hummed along the road beneath a clear blue sky.

A CSA agent was running up the steps towards the door. Tim opened it for him. The man nodded at him, "Thanks."

Tim said, "You're welcome." And walked to freedom.

Glossary

Attachment
A file that is attached to an e-mail.

CIA
Abbreviation for Central Intelligence Agency. America's Secret Service.

Coding
Instructions written in code which make up a programme.

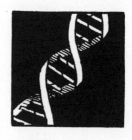

DNA
The molecule in the human body that holds the genetic information for a person. Everyone has a different DNA.

Domain Name Server

Used to map names to IP addresses. They have central lists of IP addresses and connect the domain names in Internet requests to other servers on the Internet.

Executable

A file which, when loaded onto a hard drive, can start at once without anyone telling it to do so. A file with an extension like EXE, COM, VBS is an executable. You should never open an e-mail with an attachment with one of these file names.

FSB

The Russian Secret Service (used to be known as the KGB).

Hacker
A person who tries to break through a computer or network security system.

Internet
Also known as the Net. The worldwide network that links most of the world's computers.

Into the wild
A phrase that means worms and viruses are on the Internet.

Intranet
A network of computers that can only be accessed by users who know the password (e.g. A school or a company).

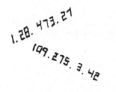

IP address
Abbreviation for Internet protocol address. This allows information to be exchanged on the Internet.

LCD
Abbreviation for Liquid Crystal Display. LCDs are used in most computers and other digital instruments.

Mac OS
A rival operating system to Windows. Developed by Apple.

MI6
The British Secret Service.

Mossad
The Israeli Secret Service.

Route
The path to use information around the Internet.

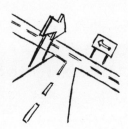

Security patches
These can change a programme so as to stop a computer virus (or worm or Trojan horse). They are often quick fixes and can be downloaded from the Internet.

Trojan horse

A computer programme that pretends to be one thing (like a game) but will really do something else (like erase a hard disk or send information to the person who sent the Trojan horse).

UNIX

A rival operating system to Windows. Developed by Bell Laboratories.

Virus

A small piece of software that can pass from computer to computer. It usually has to piggyback on top of another programme (like an e-mail) in order to work. Once it is running it can infect other documents or programmes.

Wireless Technology

The technology to connect to the Net without needing a wire or lead. It connects through radio waves.

Windows

A computer operating system devised by Microsoft.

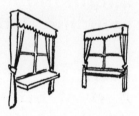

Worm

A computer programme that can copy itself from machine to machine. Worms can get into a computer through a security hole in a system or a programme.

24/7

An easy way of writing, 24 hours a day, 7 days a week. In other words, all the time.

AUTHORS' FACT FILE
STEVE BARLOW & STEVE SKIDMORE

What's your favourite computer game?

Barlow: I'm useless at computer games – I'm too slow and the baddies always chomp me while I'm wondering what to do next. I quite like puzzle games like *Myst* because I don't have to think too quickly.

Skidmore: The Tomb Raider series – highly addictive!

What's your favourite Internet Site?

Barlow and Skidmore: The *Outernet*, of course! (www.go2outer.net)

Have you ever bought anything on ebay?

Barlow: No, but I've sold stuff.

Skidmore: No.

What is the worst virus you've ever had?

Barlow: I use a Mac computer so I don't usually get viruses that affect it.

Skidmore: I got 'flu quite badly once!

Would you rather get an e-mail or a letter?

Barlow: A letter, especially one with a cheque stapled to it!

Skidmore: Depends what the letter or e-mail says!

ILLUSTRATOR FACT FILE
HARRIET BUCKLEY

What's your favourite computer game?

Myst. It's imaginative and beautiful to look at.

What's your favourite Internet Site?

Some friends of mine post strip cartoons on their weblogs, so I keep up with these when I feel like a laugh.

Have you ever bought anything on ebay?

No. I don't buy a lot online, beyond the occasional travel ticket – pretty boring really!

What is the worst virus you've ever had?

I've been lucky so far with my Mac, but I get loads of spam e-mail so I need to be on my guard.

Would you rather get an e-mail or a letter?

It depends. When you hand write a letter you can decide to do a drawing in the middle of it if you want, or you can enclose things with it. On the other hand you can send attachments with e-mails: photos, animations, web links, and that's fun too.

Barrington Stoke would like to thank all its readers for commenting on the manuscript before publication and in particular:

Riaz Ali
Saxon Allen
James Ash
Michael Athay
Conor Beasley
James Belford
Danielle Bendall
Marco Boodramsingh
Charlotte Boyd
Dean Boyle
Marc Boyle
Liz Bridge
Nicola Britton
Harry Brown
Fiona Bruce
Edward Calvert
Lucy Cavalier
Khalid Cheape
James Cliffe
Elisabeth Cotterill
Josephine Cox
Renee Devonish
Ben Dickinson
Edward Everington
Christopher Fairweather
Ashleigh Falconer
George Fleet
Raphael Gruber
Ricardo Gruber
Ryan Grundell
Robbie Gunn
Zoe Hale
Neal Hamill
Edward Hampson
Amy Handley
Ryan Handley
Shannon Hastings-Payne
Paul Hayden
Mathew Hemus
Daniel Hughes

Amir Jahangir
Esme Kirk
Fiona Kirk
Rose Kuntuala
John Lacerte
Christopher Lindop
Mattia Maccario
Liam Macdonald-Raggett
Stephen Mills
Jasmine Ndona
Mark Newton
Amy Nguyen
Georginia Nichols
Pedro Onieva
Mr S Orwin
Ismail Patel
Umar Patel
Robbie Paton
Andrew Pearce
Thomas Phillips
Ahmad Ramzan
Teresa Rich
Kelly Robin
Dominic Robinson
Lauren Robinson
Atif Sabir
Kim Sobisch
Sageer Shamim
Eleanor Seed
Natassja Shiner
Sam Silverston
Benedict Smith
Daizy Thomas
Callum Thomson
Jack Udale
Damien Wakefield
Dylan Warren
Sarah Watson-Saunders
Francesca Wood

Become a Consultant!

Would you like to give us feedback on our titles before they are published? Contact us at the e-mail address below – we'd love to hear from you!

info@barringtonstoke.co.uk   www.barringtonstoke.co.uk

Try another book in the "fyi" series!
Fiction with stacks of facts

The Environment:
Connor's Eco Den by Pippa Goodhart
Football:
Stat Man by Alan Durant
Scottish History:
Traitor's Gate by Catherine MacPhail
Space:
Space Ace by Eric Brown
The Vikings:
The Last Viking by Terry Deary

All available from our website:
www.barringtonstoke.co.uk